2-4-15 ✓

Meet Me for
Christmas
Tea

Sharyn McIntyre

Outskirts Press, Inc.
Denver, Colorado

Meet Me for Christmas Tea
All Rights Reserved.
Copyright © 2008 Sharyn McIntyre
V2.0

Illustrations by Virginia Selley All rights reserved - used with permission.

Outskirts Press, Inc.
http://www.outskirtspress.com

HB ISBN: 978-1-4327-3159-5

Library of Congress Control Number: 2008936661

Outskirts Press and the "OP" logo are trademarks belonging to Outskirts Press, Inc.

PRINTED IN THE UNITED STATES OF AMERICA

2·0·4

3 3051 00514 4609

Introduction

Meet Me for Christmas Tea

Patrick Calahan seemed quite happy and content being a bachelor until the day he found himself in the midst of a fated meeting in an airport cafe on his way home from a hectic business trip. Kandi Kayne, with her beauty, wit, and charm held him completely and hopelessly captive until she quickly and mysteriously vanished--leaving Patrick stunned with the haunting memories she left behind and the compelling and urgent desire to find her.

Kandi Kayne was a successful young woman who had found great happiness, satisfaction and joy in helping others in her career as a *Life Coach*. Her social life was like a mystical garden in full bloom overflowing with vibrant color and life. She was in no big hurry to settle down until a surprising and fateful encounter with Patrick Calahan redecorated her emotional landscape with wonder and excitement. After being mesmerized all afternoon by his charismatic personality and magnetic appeal, she suddenly realizes she is about to miss her flight and frantically dashes off in a hurried frenzy leaving him behind to anxiously wonder what it all meant.

The events that follow are filled with hope, faith, desire, and a great big dose of the spectacularly miraculous all wrapped up in a lively and colorful Christmas holiday package.

Acknowledgments

I would once again like to thank my lovely creative partner, Virginia Selley for her incredible artistic talent and intuitive perception. Her cover art and interior graphic designs are precious gifts that bless my heart and soul every time we work together. She seems to know exactly what I am looking for without a word being spoken. She is a tremendous blessing, a great friend, and a kindred spirit.

I would like to thank my wonderful family and close friends for their loving support and kindly encouragement. You are the loving springboard from which I launch every creative endeavor.

I thank Bailey, Dakota, Santana, Hank, and Tater—my beautiful horses, and Bear, Ole Red and Ole Blue-my wonderful puppies, for filling my life with unconditional love every single day. And thanks to all my kitties—they constantly show me that taking time out to play is a vitally important part of life.

I thank God from whom all my blessings miraculously flow.

Dedication

I would like to dedicate this book to *God*, my *Guardian Angels* and *Heavenly Guides* who whisper softly into my spirit the creative ideas and special messages that find their way here to sweetly grace the pages of my books. I am simply a willing vessel through which a greater message flows. This would not be happening without you.

I thank you sincerely and wholeheartedly for your unconditional love, omnipotent guidance and infinite patience.

Chapter 1

Kandi Kayne at twenty-nine still found it amusing to hear her name called over the airport intercom. Her mother being absolutely obsessed with Christmas had no doubt found her inspiration for naming her only offspring from her exceptional love for the magical holiday.

She frantically rushed to retrieve her message from the airline desk and found it most disappointing to discover that her friend Jackie, whom she had not seen in quite some time, was delayed by a work-related emergency and would not be able to meet her for lunch while she awaited her connecting flight back to the Wilmington International Airport.

As she approached the crowded airport café she was contemplating how she would fill the next several hours now that her friend would not be joining her to keep her company while she waited. It was the perfect opportunity to catch up after such a long time and she was a bit saddened that it had not worked out as planned, although she perfectly understood that there are no mistakes and it was obviously not meant to happen at this time.

She quickly slid into the only remaining booth available and was quite relieved to have at least found a place to settle in while she waited for the time to pass before her final leg of the journey back home. She ordered a cup of *"Christmas Tea"* as the advertisement leaped off the pages of the menu to quickly and delightfully grab her attention.

The café was perfectly dressed in the *Spirit of Christmas* and as she took in the holiday decorations all around her, she found her thoughts drifting back to the previous several days spent in New York City with her long-time friends from all the way back to high school days. They had spent three absolutely glorious days together taking in the sights, sounds, tastes and smells of the *"Big Apple"* while laughing, reminiscing, Christmas shopping, and enjoying the enchanting Christmas shows before parting at the airport with hugs and heart-felt Christmas wishes. It would be another long year before they found themselves together again, and Kandi laughed as she recalled how spectacularly they had made the best of their annual Christmas gathering once again.

As she took her first sip of the nostalgic holiday beverage served in a festive, seasonal Christmas cup she was delighted with the old familiar taste that seemed to bring a flood of *yuletide memories* of special moments spent with dear ones celebrating the holidays, while she eagerly perused the colorfully decorated holiday menu before her with enthusiastic anticipation.

Kandi was happy to have been able to take a welcome break from her busy schedule to spend time with her dearest and most cherished friends.

As another year quickly approached the end it had proven to be a busy one and her career as a *"Life Coach"* had taken off like a rocket-blast. Her appointment book was completely bulging with appointments with clients and she found that helping others discover their gifts and talents had been so amazingly fulfilling and rewarding as a career choice. It had been an extraordinary year for which she found herself truly in a state of thanksgiving and gratitude.

As her eyes wandered enthusiastically all over the menu she heard an unfamiliar voice surprisingly addressing her. "Excuse me, Miss, may I sit? There seems to be no available seats left in this place and I have quite a wait for my connecting flight. Would you mind terribly if I joined you?" She quickly dropped the menu and took in the sight of a most handsome man as he reached out his hand to her. "Mr. Calahan here, but if you allow me to sit for a bit and rest my weary bones you may certainly call me Patrick," he said with a laugh.

"Please sit down Mr. Calahan; I surely wouldn't want your weary bones wearing out all over the airport cafe, now would I Sir? What a mess that might turn out to be," she responded with a smile. "My name is Miss Kayne, but you Sir, may call me Kandi since it is Christmas and I'm feeling most particularly in a state of holiday cheer."

As she observed the clear signs of humorously displayed skepticism all over his face, she assured him, "No, I am perfectly serious Mr. Calahan; Kandi Kayne is my real name —it's a long story—let's don't go there!" And they both chuckled as he made himself comfortable across from her in the café booth and was much better able to scrutinize her obvious attractiveness and apparent beauty despite the fact that her name sounded like something out of an animated Christmas movie.

"Well, actually, it seems I do have time for a long story this afternoon Miss Kayne, with an unfortunate layover to catch my connecting flight back to New Mexico. I would imagine it has been an interesting life with a name like Kandi Kayne. I suspect that you are constantly assuring people that you are not kidding," he said with a chuckle. "Oh, I am always kidding Mr. Calahan; I find it particularly amusing, but not about my name."

"You may call me Patrick, Miss Kayne," he repeated. "And, you Sir, may call me Kandi, Mr. Calahan," she quickly responded as they both laughed out loud, perfectly aware that neither of them had any intentions of giving in first.

"What do you do, Mr. Calahan?" She asked inquisitively. "Just about everything I possibly can, and if I find it particularly satisfying, stimulating, interesting, and amusing, I make sure I find the time to do it again as often as I can. When there's time left over, I work as a Quantum Physicist. Now how's that for a surprise, huh? I mean, if you even know what that might be," he laughed as he saw the look of absolute shock take over her entire face as she couldn't possibly hide her astonishment.

"Wow, I am particularly fascinated with Quantum Physics myself, Mr. Calahan," she stated quite matter-of-factly. And, just when he was convinced that she undoubtedly had to be putting him on, she added, "Quantum Physics....yes, I know what that might be—a discrete quantity of electro-magnetic energy—the stuff our entire world is made of when we reduce it back down to its bare essence."

Now he was the one staring blankly with shock and surprise to her absolute amusement.

"How is it at all likely that someone who looks like you could possibly be into such serious science?" He laughed. "Oh the world is full of surprises, Mr. Calahan, don't you find that to be true?" She responded with a smile that lit up the café and allowed him to closely observe the lovely dimples in her flawless cheeks that made her beautiful smile absolutely and incandescently irresistible.

" Since you are indeed a Quantum Physicist, Mr. Calahan, perhaps someday in the future you will discover a way to explain the holographic nature of what we observe in the quantum universe, as well as what we see in our everyday world, and formulate equations to unify the explanations into one consistent story. We've come quite a way from Newtonian Physics of the late 1600's. Field-Theory Physics, Quantum Physics, Relativity Physics, and String-Theory Physics—the big question is, "What's in the space between all the space? And if it's empty, wouldn't that be an awful waste of space?" She asked.

5

"Stop it! Miss Kayne, I'm going to give you about three decades to quit dazzling me with your metaphysical charms." He laughed and continued, "You do surprise and delight me with your question! The truth of the matter is modern science may have discovered what's inside the empty space: a field of energy that is different from any other form of energy. This energy appears to be everywhere, always and to have existed since the very beginning of time. I happen to believe that within this energy is the existence of an intelligent mind responsible for our physical world, and it joins everything together connected at the source. And, since we are all made up of this energy, and connected by this energy, once something is joined it is always connected whether it remains physically linked or not. Modern experiments strongly suggest that regardless of how much space separates two things, once joined they are always connected energy-wise," he concluded.

"Ah, Mr. Calahan, Einstein must be turning over in his grave about now, as he certainly believed all the way to the time of his death that the universe existed separate from us."

"Yes, Miss Kayne, but by now surely the ole fart knows better," he replied with a chuckle, as she easily and quite comfortably joined him in laughter.

The waitress was rather hesitant to even approach the table as it was practically impossible to interrupt their conversation that seemed to have no end in sight. When she finally found a break, she asked Patrick if he was ready to order. "What are you having Miss Kayne?" He curiously questioned. "I'm having a cup of Christmas Tea, Mr. Calahan—tis the season." He smiled and requested, "Bring me one of those too, and make it a double." And the three of them laughed together as the waitress assured him it was coming right up.

The afternoon seemed to slip by unnoticed as the two of them bantered back and forth in a continuing discussion of the cosmos from every possible angle, and a confession from both that even with all the newly found discoveries in the world of science, both of them held fast to their long-cherished Christian beliefs and ideals and actually found no discrepancies, but further evidence that science was indeed catching up with what the *Holy Scriptures* had written long ago.

Several cups of *"Christmas Tea"* later, following a platter of mixed appetizers, many laughs and humorous ex-changes, Patrick excused himself to go to the men's room. Kandi was happy to have a quiet moment as the time had gone by so quickly with very little break between their quick exchanges that she hadn't had time to gather her thoughts about this unusual meeting. "Sometimes life dishes up some pretty incredible and amazing surprises and experiences," she thought, "and this is certainly one of those times."

Just then she glanced for the first time all afternoon at the time on her cell phone and somewhat frantically realized she was about to miss her flight! She only had five minutes to get to the terminal and board the plane. Without even thinking, she quickly opened her wallet, threw three twenty dollar bills down on the table along with one of her busi-ness cards, grabbed her bag and hurriedly ran from the café not noticing at all that in her haste, her bag had swiped the business card off the table and under the booth as she shouted to her waitress, "I left the money on the table—I'm about to miss my flight. Please tell Mr. Calahan that I'm sorry."

To say that Patrick was frustrated when he returned to find her gone is an understatement. He questioned the waitress adamantly and was sorely disappointed that she could give him no further information concerning this amazing young woman who quite suddenly disappeared from his life as quickly and surprisingly as she came. He didn't even know where she lived and found himself to be quite sorry that he had left those questions unspoken.

As he checked his watch he realized his flight was leaving in twenty minutes and he quickly made his way to the terminal to board. All along the way he looked around him in the hopes of catching a glimpse of this fascinating creature that had come into his life so unexpectedly and held him completely captive with her beauty, wit, charm and intelligence, but despite his energetic and determined efforts, he found no sight of her. He felt like shouting her name all through the airport in the hopes of miraculously finding her again, but quickly realized how ridiculous that would be to run around shouting

"Candy Cane"—"they'd probably lock me up as some kind of psychologically deranged Christmas nut!" He laughed.

He boarded the plane and took his seat. As he gazed out the window overlooking the runway that was about to whisk him away and return him to the west, the memories of her smile, her dimples, her beautiful green eyes that seemed to mesmerize him and pull him inside her filled every crevice of his mind, and the realization that she was gone hit him again as a sadness swiftly washed over his spirit. "I've got to find her!" He thought. "I've just got to find her!"

Kandi was finally in the air and happy to be homebound. She glanced down at the white puffy clouds that decorated the heavenly landscape escorting her home and settled into her seat to reflect upon the afternoon. "This kind of thing happens so rarely and I know it's no coincidence that Jackie couldn't meet me today. This was a fated meeting. He could very well be the one I have waited all my life to meet. I've got to hear from him again! I've just got to hear from him again," she thought, as she gazed out the window and wondered if she would ever be fortunate enough to see him again.

Chapter 2

After a relatively smooth flight home, Kandi's plane finally landed and she made her way to the baggage claim area to retrieve her luggage. She was physically tired, but still emotionally reeling from the pleasurable trip and exciting encounter with Patrick Calahan.

She felt the caresses of the Sun on her face as she walked to the long term parking section catching lovely glimpses of the very beginning moments of the sunset as she filled her trunk with the remains of her delightful and long anticipated Christmas trip.

As the sounds of the engine fired, the radio station was playing "Love is the Answer" and as she listened to the lyrics and moving melody she found herself wishing more than ever before that her true soul mate would find his way to her—home for Christmas where he belonged—snuggled in front of a beautifully lit Christmas tree enjoying a romantic first Christmas together.

She eagerly pulled out of the airport exit and began her final part of the journey back to Topsail Island. As she made her way through the traffic, she could hardly wait to reach home so she could quietly reflect upon the amazing events of the past week without interruption or distraction.

Her parents had built the lovely home on the sound side of the island many years before and when Kandi graduated from college with a Masters in Psychology they signed over the deed as a gift for their appreciation of her hard work, dedication and accomplishments.

The house was perfectly nestled into the center of a cul-de-sac that majestically kissed the back water where an enchanting sunset graced her back deck every clear evening to her absolute delight and entertainment. The upper deck just outside of the glass doors located off of her living-dining area had long been a place of inspiration allowing her to easily imagine her most beautiful and magical dreams.

She stood at the triple French doors gazing out to the water to steal a quick gaze before the evening flawlessly surrendered to nightfall. She was happy to be home again. She poured herself a glass of Chardonnay and found her way to the couch where she thankfully flopped, resting her feet upon the coffee table as she took in a deep breath, followed by a sigh of relief, and settled back to reminisce about the events of the week.

She laughed to herself as she recalled the afternoon spent in the airport café and wondered if she would ever hear from Patrick Calahan again. She was thankful that in her frantic hurry she was careful to leave her business card on the table—hoping that he had enjoyed the afternoon as much as she did—enough to perhaps want to do it again sometime in the very near future.

She noticed her phone was flashing with messages which abruptly pulled her back to the present moment as she enthusiastically pushed the button to listen. Her parents had left a *welcome home* message from their pleasurable retreat in the beautiful Appalachian mountains of Western Maryland where they contentedly spent their summers, as well as a few visits during the winter months. They asked her to return their call when she had time to share the events of her trip. The second message was from her long-time friend Stacy whose parents built the house next door. They played together since they were young girls enjoying the summers on the island. Stacy sounded quite excited as she listened to her message, "Kandi, this is Stacy—call me girlfriend; I can't wait to hear all about your Christmas trip and I want the scoop, nothing but the scoop so help you God! Welcome home! I missed you terribly. Either call me or get yourself over here!"

Kandi and Stacy had learned to sail together many years before and after many sailing lessons, Stacy had decided the previous summer to purchase a beautiful thirty foot sail boat that had everything including the kitchen sink onboard which provided them with many relaxing weekends enjoying the crystal clear waters of Topsail Island as they mulled over the pleasures, joys and struggles of life decidedly determined to try their very best to solve all the problems of the world each time they found themselves out on the water together.

Kandi smiled as she realized how very thankful she was to

Meet Me for Christmas Tea

have been blessed with such good friends in her life. Stacy was very similar in temperament and they had shared many of their greatest desires, secrets and ambitions through the years. There wasn't much that Stacy didn't know about Kandi, and vice-versa. She couldn't wait to tell her about Patrick Calahan and the seemingly fated afternoon she spent with him that day.

Stacy had found her perfect match several years before and they had married early in the fall, prior to moving into her parent's summer home that they had surprisingly presented to her and her husband Chris as a wedding gift. Chris was a very successful building contractor and Stacy was a professional photographer. They made wonderful neighbors and seemed much more like family than dear friends.

Kandi recalled the beautiful day of their wedding and re-membered as she helped Stacy get ready to walk down that aisle of love and commitment—the moment just before it was time to begin the ceremony when Stacy looked at her with sparkling eyes of happiness, winked at her and whis-pered, "You're next!" She remembered thinking, "I hope so, because I am ready to find my Mister Right." She couldn't help but feel that he was closer than he'd ever been before. As she looked out the windows to the mag-nificently star-filled, clear winter sky she wondered who he was-- where he was—what he was doing—and hoped that he was looking up to the same shining bright stars and wishing for her as much as she was longing and wishing for him.

Kandi had a few relationships in the past that held her at-tention for a time but as the relationships progressed it be-came more and more apparent that their differences far

13

outweighed any similarities of interest and the personality conflicts were just too much to overcome. They had ended on a friendly note with no regrets as she found every experience in life to be of worth for one reason or another and moved on peacefully without a backward glance fully knowing and wholeheartedly believing that someone quite exceptional was in her future and when the time was perfectly right, he would magically find his way to her without being a fraction of a second late.

After she returned her parent's call and delightfully recounted the highlights of her week, deliberately leaving the last part out to avoid further questions, she decided to run next door and deliver Stacy the scoop that she sounded so desperate to hear in her phone message.

She bounced down the steps and quickly made her way next door. With a loud knock, she opened the front door and yelled "Hello up there—I hope nobody's naked because I'm coming up the steps—so if this is not a good time speak now or forever hold your fully clothed peace. I've got the scoop and I'm here to deliver it—ready or not!"

With that she heard the excited voice of her dear friend running to greet her with a great big grin. As she reached the top of the stairs Kandi reached out her arms as Stacy embraced her with a loving hug that was so familiar and welcoming. "Get in here girl, and tell me all about your Christmas trip! Was it fun? Did you have a good time? And what did you get me?" Stacy laughed as she made her way to the fridge to get her friend a glass of her favorite wine, and Kandi sat by the window staring out at the beautiful night as she contemplated where she should begin.

After telling her all about her New York City adventure, she saved the best for last, and Stacy could tell that she was withholding something particular by the mysterious look on her face and the gleam in her eyes. "And now I have to tell you girl, I had the most extraordinary meeting at the airport as I waited for my connecting flight. I met an unusual man by the name of Patrick Calahan. I can't remember when I have ever been quite so taken by a personality," she said, as she observed the excitement rising in Stacy's facial expression. "Well for heaven's sake, tell me about him promptly before I frantically pop my bulging cork in anticipation," Stacy blurted, as a hefty giggle broke through her magnanimous enthusiasm.

For the next half hour Kandi recalled the events of the afternoon and shared them with her dear friend who discreetly held all of her secrets since childhood days. They laughed like two little girls again and recalled the time that little Travis Benson and his family moved into the rental house down the street one summer for the week and how the two of them had giggled over him the entire week he was there each and every time they saw him, wondering where he came from, and trying to imagine him as their grown up prince charming who would ride up on his magnificent white stallion some enchanting day and delightfully carry one of them off into the sunset to live gloriously happy-ever-after.

Stacy was thrilled to hear Kandi's recollection of the unexpected afternoon encounter and the two of them teasingly tossed tantalizing scenarios back and forth laughing as they dreamed and imagined together what might possibly happen next.

Chapter 3

Patrick's plane landed right on schedule and he was delighted to find his good friend, Kelly waiting as he made his way out the front doors of the Albuquerque International Airport. It had been a hectic business trip with long, though interesting seminars and meetings, and it felt quite good to be home again in the midst of familiar surroundings and a wonderfully friendly face. He was looking forward to the short drive back to Santa Fe to catch up with his closest friend.

As he thanked Kelly for picking him up, his friend couldn't help but notice that something seemed different about Patrick. Even after a busy week and journey back home he seemed unusually invigorated. "You must have had an enjoyable trip. I can see it all over you, Man," he declared.

"Well, the business was just okay, but the afternoon I spent with a tantalizing candy cane on the way back was the absolute highlight of the whole trip," he answered with a chuckle. "Hmmmmmm, I didn't realize you were a particular fan of candy canes there, Buddy." "Oh let me assure you that I have never had the pleasure of a candy cane quite like this one, my friend," he laughed. "Well, do tell me more about this candy cane then as you have certainly peeked my curiosity and interest. It must be made from some pretty incredible ingredients to have had such a positive effect on you, Pal."

"Well, let's see, she was about five feet-six inches, give or take a half an inch with beautiful dark hair cascading in soft little curls all the way down her back, with gorgeous green eyes, dimples to die for that were perfectly placed on the cheeks of the most beautiful face I have ever laid eyes upon in my entire life, and that face was connected to a body that was utterly alluring to say the least—and besides being incredibly beautiful she is smart, funny, and absolutely, downright irresistible. Believe it or not, her name is Kandi Kayne, and yes my friend, that is her real name, she positively assured me."

"Wow, she sounds like something out of a fairytale there Buddy, exactly what were you drinking on your way home there, eh? Were they serving doubles in the airport lounge?" Patrick laughed and replied, "I know how it sounds, but I can promise you that I am not even slightly exaggerating –the problem is….she slipped away before I even found out where she lives. I don't really know anything personal about her other than her unusual name, and that she was waiting for a connecting flight to somewhere, and I was fortunate enough to have the pleasure of spending half the afternoon with her before she vanished. If it's the last thing I ever do, I am going to find her, and that you can count on," he stated quite matter-of-factly.

"Unless she has some serious character flaws and a scandalous or criminal background that I am not yet aware of at this time, I think I have found the woman of my dreams and I intend to ride this horse all the way back to the campfire, my good friend," he laughed.

Kelly smiled as he could see quite clearly that his friend had definitely had an encounter with someone quite impressive. He'd never seen him quite so enthusiastic about a female, although there had been a few in his past that captured his interest temporarily, but couldn't seem to hold his attention for very long.

They chatted about the weather and the local news while he was gone and before long they were pulling into the driveway of Patrick's patio home deeply nestled outside the city limits of the beautiful Santa Fe landscape. Kelly lived across the street with his wife Anastasia, whom they affectionately called Ana and they had been neighbors for five years. He and his wife owned a charming little café in the city which kept them quite busy, and Patrick was a frequent visitor with a favorite table by the front windows overlooking the busy, crowded street. It was a perfect place to *"people-watch"* which was one of his favorite pastimes.

Kelly and Ana were like family to him. Both of his parents had passed on and his only sister lived on the east coast with her husband and four children. He didn't get to see them as often as he would like, so it was quite nice to have an extended family close by.

As he took his bags from the car, he walked around to the driver's side window, patted Kelly on the shoulder and said, "Thanks Man, I appreciate the ride home. I owe ya one!

I'll come by the restaurant tomorrow for dinner and buy ya a beer. Thank Ana for me, for lending me her favorite bartender for a bit, I owe her one too!"

"You're welcome, Buddy, anytime! See ya tomorrow," he said as he smoothly shifted into reverse and pulled out of the driveway.

Patrick flopped his bags down in the master bedroom and made his way to the kitchen where he grabbed a cold beer and decided to head out back for a soak in the hot tub. It was his favorite way to top off any day. It was always nice to gain a few hours on the clock upon the return of an east coast trip, and the Sun was just setting on the cozy brick patio.

As he sank into the hot, steamy water he felt himself truly relax and begin to unwind.

As he twisted the cap off of his beer and took his first gulp he couldn't help but smile as he remembered that just a few hours before he was sitting in a café drinking *Christmas Tea*—something he had never had before, and he couldn't help but wish that he was still there with her in the cozy little booth, looking into those magnetic green eyes—taking in her smile—listening to her laughter—catching the lovely fragrance from her beautiful, long, dark, shiny hair as she turned her head occasionally—a scent that would haunt his memory as it deeply embedded itself somewhere inside his emotions for safe keeping.

He remembered her teal green sweater and how it brought out the magnificent color of her eyes and made them positively mesmerizing as he completely lost himself in them for several hours while she quite easily held him entirely captive there.

He looked deeply out into the glorious Santa Fe sunset and promised himself that he would find her again. He found himself wondering what she was doing at that moment. "Is she thinking of me, too," he thought. "Did she enjoy their little *Christmas Tea Party* as much as he had? " He wondered.

He was surprised to be able to sincerely, honestly, and openly confess that he was completely captivated by her. He was more than ready to find his perfect match, and he realized it even more after having the delightful pleasure of spending the afternoon with the perfectly lovely and mysterious Kandi Kayne. He was most eager and curious to see what would happen next and how long it would take as he sat back to contemplate what the future would possibly bring for them.

Chapter 4

K andi woke after a relatively good night's sleep and as she was in the midst of pouring her first cup of freshly brewed coffee of the day she recalled a dream she'd had during the night that brought chill bumps as the memory of it hauntingly returned.

She was sitting in a very familiar restaurant in St. Augustine, Florida where she and Stacy had traveled many times through the years. It was truly one of her favorite places to visit and vacation, as her favorite Aunt Grace lived there. She immediately recognized the familiar place as she curiously looked around her.

In the dream she was sitting at their favorite table by the front window and she was enthusiastically taking in the view of the cozy little brick street just outside. She noticed that Christmas decorations were all around the restaurant and holiday garland lined the windows. Soft white lights whispered a sweet holiday message of good cheer as they beautifully decorated a little tree that sat out front next to a lovely trickling water fountain, and candles flickered softly on the tables as the touch of fine linen brushed across her hand while she reached for a cup in front of her—taking in the aroma of cinnamon and spice *Christmas Tea* that filled the air.

She noticed that she felt anxious about the arrival of someone that she seemed to be waiting for as she sat there taking in the holiday atmosphere. She caught a glimpse of a tall figure making his way quickly down the cozy brick street toward the restaurant. The closer he got the more she began to recognize him—it was Patrick Calahan! She could feel the rhythm of her heartbeat begin to accelerate as he swiftly grew closer and closer, and just as he reached the front door to enter, she woke—startled. She remembered sitting up in bed as she felt the lively pounding beats of her heart, and quickly realized it was only a dream.

"I've got to get a grip here," she thought. "This mysterious man is really doing a number on my psyche!"

She gathered herself, walked over to the glass doors and peeked outside to the fresh beginnings of a beautiful new day that seemed to be ever- so- sweetly calling her name. She loved how beautiful the water was, especially in the winter months—a beautiful bluish-green Caribbean color and she ardently watched as a family of pelicans glided overhead in the crisp morning sky in hot pursuit of their very own unique version of breakfast.

She was happy that she had blocked out the week on her

appointment schedule to finish her Christmas preparations and get into the kitchen to do some holiday baking. Christmas Eve was rapidly approaching. It was her absolute favorite holiday of the year and she looked quite forward to it all year through. Her childhood memories came back like a refreshing flood at this special time of year, and she found that she felt happiest and most positive when she was surrounded by all the reminders of her charming *Christmas Past.*

As she glanced at the calendar hanging on the inside door of her pantry, she suddenly realized that the yearly wrapping party that she and Stacy hosted each year was coming up that evening. They always invited a group of girlfriends over to gather around the big dining area table for an evening of fun and sharing. Each person was required to bring two special holiday treats to share with the group, along with the recipes written out for each to take home, and their final Christmas packages they hadn't gotten around to wrapping yet, along with the decorative wrap, bows and name tags. They made an amusing assembly line around the table and wrapped their presents together while sipping *Christmas Tea* and telling their favorite stories pulled from their beloved yuletide memory banks of old. It was always a fun evening, and a productive way to get the job done while classic Christmas carols played softly and nostalgically in the background to the delight and entertainment of all those lucky enough to be present around the table each year.

She decided she better get busy before the day surprisingly got away from her, as they often did during this busy time of year. She earnestly made her way to the kitchen to pull out her recipe box to decide what tantalizing Christmas creations she would lovingly prepare to share with the girls that evening.

As she walked to the kitchen, she noticed the cordless phone sitting on the countertop and stopped to stare for a moment—wondering if Patrick would make good use of the business card she'd left him on the table and decide to call her sometime over the holidays. She paused a bit to thoroughly enjoy that moment of thought. She had long ago learned the importance of bringing more consciousness into her life even in the most ordinary situations. She believed it helped one to grow in "presence power" as it generates a field around us of high vibrational frequency and just as darkness cannot survive in the presence of light, no negativity, or discord can present itself and survive when one is fully present in the moment and completely at ease within oneself. She believed we are all responsible for our own inner space and peace, and it was a choice each moment to walk in gratitude, hope, faith, and the thrill of endless possibility. She felt the excitement rise within her as she contemplated the prospect of that phone call and all the opportunity it might magically deliver right along with it.

She made a choice long ago to be happy within herself and by herself. She had no need for ego-based attachments, and was perfectly willing to wait for that relationship where true love could wonderfully and miraculously flourish and she knew perfectly well that in order to experience it from the outside, it was imperative for her to thoroughly and completely experience it from the inside first. The more she learned to be present within herself, in love, and complete acceptance, the quicker she would draw that relationship that perfectly mirrored the peace, joy and love she found within. She was fully aware that true communication is communion with another; the realization of oneness, which is love. It is a Divine process and she trusted it to deliver all that she needs and right on time. She had a complete grasp on the fact that God is never late, but His timing is perfect. "There is great peace to be found in that," she earnestly believed.

After enjoying the notion of all those marvelous possibilities and following it as far as she could, ending with an earnest prayer of faith, she joyfully flipped through her recipes to begin the task at hand, deciding to enjoy every moment of the day and all of the tastes, smells and sights of what would magically come forth from her warm, waiting oven to share with her delightful friends. "This was going to be an exceedingly good day--followed by a host of many others," she decided wholeheartedly.

Chapter 5

P atrick was always upbeat and energetic in the mornings—excited at the prospects and possibilities of a brand new day.

As he glanced toward the clock on his nightstand he was surprised to find that he actually slept until six-thirty. It was quite unusual for him to sleep late. Ordinarily he was up and moving around quite actively by six in the morning—even on weekends.

He then noticed the pile of boxes sitting by the dresser all painstakingly packaged in holiday style and ready to be express- mailed to his sister Caroline and her family for Christmas. He decided matter-of-factly to place that job first on the list of the accomplishments for the day—after morning coffee and a refreshing shower, of course.

As he eagerly made his way to the kitchen to get the coffee

started he remembered a strange dream that woke him in the night. He wasn't at all surprised that the mysterious Kandi Kayne would haunt him in his dreams and he laughed to himself as he realized what a profound effect that young woman had obviously had on him.

In the dream he was in a strange place and couldn't quite focus on his surroundings to correctly identify them. What he did recognize perfectly was a lovely little Italian-looking restaurant decorated for Christmas on a vintage brick street with a lovely water fountain outside the front door, and the majestic sight of Miss Kandi Kayne as he entered this strange place that seemed encapsulated in a dreamy fog. She was superbly seated at a table surrounded by a mysterious mist and she was smiling as if she was waiting there just for him—delighted by his arrival. Before he could reach her—he woke—quite suddenly and immediately felt the little bits of disappointment that quickly followed when he realized it was only a dream. "I'll have to finish that dream later when I can devote more attention, time and energy to it because I definitely want to follow through and find the pot of gold at the end of that particularly lovely rainbow," he chuckled.

Patrick had become accustomed to being a bachelor and although he was hoping to find a life partner to share in his greatest wishes, hopes and dreams, he was content to enjoy his life everyday as best he could, always being open to the realm of possibility without placing limits or narrow boundaries on what incredible experiences could surprisingly unfold before him. He felt that every day was an opportunity to bring him something extraordinarily miraculous and he made it a point to be careful to make sure his door was always open to whatever wonderful possibilities may lie ahead.

He had surrendered long ago to the simple yet profound wisdom of *yielding* to, rather than *opposing* the natural flow of life. He believed that there is something within us that remains unaffected by the transient circumstances that make up our life situation, and only through surrender do we have access to it. It is our lives, our very *BEING* which exists eternally in the timeless realm of the present. Finding this life was one of the great messages of Jesus.

During times when he found his life unsatisfactory he realized it was only in surrendering first that he would break the unconscious resistance pattern that perpetuated the situation. He perfectly understood that surrender is compatible with taking action, initiating change or achieving our life goals. But it is in the surrender state that a totally different energy—a different quality flows into our doing. It reconnects us to our Source-God and in that state we become infused with His energy, and a joyful celebration of life-force energy springs forth into our now—therefore the quality of whatever we are doing or creating becomes immeasurably enhanced. The results will then look after themselves and reflect that Divine Source quality right into our every day reality.

It was this profound realization and belief that allowed him to perfectly trust that all is well with him and that his mate would one day become a part of his life experience because it was truly a heart's desire. Until the manifestation became apparent, he would choose to enjoy his life alone as best he could, always open and willing—keenly ready for the miraculous to unfold.

As his thoughts moved back to the afternoon before, he couldn't help but feel as if his sudden encounter with Kandi Kayne was the very beginnings of this manifestation, and that as the days ahead began to open up, he would indeed see more and more of the unfolding taking place before him. It was that comforting thought that served as the motivational wind beneath his sails beckoning him onward like a loving springboard to get positively moving with his day.

After dropping off the packages at the post office, he decided to make his way over to the café to see if there was anything he could do to help Kelly and Ana. He was happy that his schedule was clear until the New Year. It had been a busy year, with lots of travel, meetings, seminars, and projects, and he was happy to take a breather to wrap up an eventful and successful year.

As he walked into the café he was greeted with a welcome hug from Ana who comically held an expression on her face like she had been surreptitiously given access to his deepest held and most cherished secrets—and was about to spill them into the center of the café like an overflowing dam after a fearsome flood. "Why are you looking at me like that?" He laughed. "Oh, it's nothing," she replied with a big grin. "Oh come now, Miss Anastasia, that doesn't at all look like nothing to me!" He laughed.

With that, she reached into her pocket and pulled out a candy cane, slipping it cheerfully into his shirt pocket, and disappeared into the kitchen, as he heard her call out to Kelly, "Sweetheart, your love-struck cohort is here!" And he couldn't help but burst into laughter.

Shortly thereafter his smiling friend appeared behind the

bar and insisted on buying him a beer. "I see my secrets are no longer safe with you my pathetically loose-lipped friend," Patrick chuckled. " Well, I simply told her there was a new recipe floating around for magical candy canes that had the uncanny ability to make one giddy, and ridiculously happy with jovial holiday spirit. I can't help that she insisted upon knowing the recipe and I told her she would have to get it from you," he laughed. "She pretty much figured it out on her own without much help from me," he added. "Oh sure she did—remind me to keep my secret, covert candy recipes to myself from now on," he replied as they both let out a hearty laugh.

"Before I have that beer, I'd like to help you guys around here some. Is there anything you need done that I can help you with my shamelessly indiscreet object of betrayal?" "Well, there's always something that needs done around here… Dr. Love… Prince Charming….Mister Romance…. let me find Ana and see what is most pressing and if you can concentrate on something other than candy canes for a little while, we'll go from there," he laughed again.

As his friend disappeared into the kitchen, Patrick looked around the café and thought of how much fun it would be to some day introduce Kandi to his dearest friends. As one thought led to another he was filled with joy at the emotions that were being stirred within until Kelly reappeared from behind the kitchen doors and interrupted his lovely daydreams with a pending chore. "Ana would like for you to string some white lights in the front window, if you don't mind," he questioned. "If Miss Anastasia wants lights in the front window—that is exactly what she is going to get," he laughed. And with that Kelly placed his arm around his shoulder and thankfully led him to the storeroom to help him get started.

Before long the formerly bare window was all aglow with festive white lights that seemed to whisper a soft and sweet "*Merry Christmas*" to their guests as they entered and a satisfied Patrick—for a job well-done, took a seat at the bar to cash in on the previous beer offer. As he settled into his seat and relaxed, looking around at the Christmas decorations all over the café, he felt exceptionally happy and content, like the little boy who excitedly went to bed on Christmas Eve, fully expecting and anticipating the joys of finding that long awaited, perfectly wonderful gift under the tree the next morning. A tiny smile graced his grateful lips seemingly coming from a deep place inside, and he suddenly felt incredibly thankful for….whatever was to come.

Chapter 6

K andi was content to find herself alone in front of the quaintly decorated Christmas tree filled with sparkling white lights that were shining like dazzling diamonds bouncing and reflecting all over the cozy room.

It was always nice when Christmas Eve arrived, and all the shopping, wrapping, baking and work was behind her for another holiday season. Now she could take a deep breath and truly relax.

Her parents would be arriving in the morning for Christmas brunch and Kandi had already prepared a scrumptious breakfast casserole that she could pop into the oven in the morning when they arrived, along with a delicious coffee cake she had just taken from the warm oven.

She had purposely declined several Christmas Eve parties

and gatherings to spend the evening in quiet reflection accompanied by her favorite Christmas carols playing softly in the background— with her favorite wine in a lovely red, long stemmed crystal glass, as she enjoyed the company of all of her old, nostalgic Christmas tree ornaments beautifully displayed before her like friends from her past singing sweet songs of delightful holiday memories with lovely melodies of days gone by. A bayberry candle earnestly shared its fragrant scent filling the room as it flickered ever-so- gently on the coffee table. The gas logs in the rustic stone fireplace were all aglow as the flames danced a lovely yuletide waltz that put the finishing touches on the cozy, festive portrait that graced the room and brought the *Spirit of Christmas* fully to life once again.

Her thoughts repeatedly returned to the afternoon in the airport café, as she wished she was sharing the wonderful feeling of holiday cheer with that special someone she'd waited all her life to meet.

Her magnificent memories of childhood Christmas were usually enough to help her sail through the holidays in magical wonder and excitement, but this year she was feeling an emptiness that she hadn't experienced before, as if suddenly reaching a fresh new awareness that something significant was missing from this beautiful picture before her, and it was time to redecorate her life with something new and perfectly amazing to complete this personal portrait that cried out to be finished.

She couldn't help but wonder why Patrick hadn't called. "Perhaps he wasn't as interested as he seemed and maybe I made much more out of this than he did," she thought.

Just then, the phone rang and she just about jumped completely out of her skin as it jolted her from her thoughts unexpectedly. She dared to hope once more as the phone rang the second time and she reached to remove it from its cradle. The caller ID stole her excitement in a flash as Stacy's number quickly appeared, and though she was always happy to hear from her dear friend, she couldn't help but feel the let down. "Merry Christmas Stac," she answered, trying to hide her touch of disappointment. "Hey Kandi! Merry Christmas! I just wanted to ask you one more time if you wanted to join us over here. We have quite a houseful as you can probably hear and see from your windows. Chris' entire family is over here and they are about to break out the instruments and play some holiday music. You know we'd really love it if you'd join us," she stated sincerely.

"I appreciate it so much Honey, I really do, but I would truly like to take this special evening and spend it alone. I'm not upset or depressed, or anything like that, so don't worry, okay? I just feel like enjoying the quiet and the peace. I've spent so many years partying on Christmas Eve, and I thoroughly enjoyed each one, but this year, I am feeling very drawn to the spiritual side of the holiday and I'd like to just spend it with *HIM*, in thanksgiving, gratitude and appreciation. I just don't do that enough anymore. So you all have yourselves a wonderful Christmas Eve, and I'm sure I'll see you tomorrow sometime. Come over when you get a chance. I have a surprise from New York City for you!" She finished.

"Ah, you can count on it, Miss Kayne. I have a surprise for you too. I'll see ya later. Enjoy your Christmas Eve, and put in a good word for us with the Big Guy, although we're getting ready to play and sing some of His favorite tunes," she kidded.

"I'll be sure to do that," she laughed, and softly hung up the phone.

As she settled back into her comfortable chair, she sipped her wine as her eyes caught sight of the manger scene on the fireplace mantel as it tenderly drew her attention. She flashed back to *"Christmas Past"* when the excitement of Santa Claus was a bit overwhelming, but yet she was always spiritually and sentimentally drawn to the sight of the manger scene, and the memories of being on her knees beside her bed before climbing in to strain and struggle with the notorious *Sand Man* who had no trouble arriving any other night, but on Christmas Eve he was nowhere to be found when you needed him most. It was in the midst of the restless tossing and turning where she always seemed to find her way to Jesus and his precious Christmas gift, and it was there that the peacefulness of sleep would finally settle upon her.

She recalled the overwhelming feelings of thankfulness as she looked at the baby Jesus, wrapped in swaddling clothes sleeping peacefully in the manger and quickly walked out His life from that moment in her heart and spirit, realizing the gloriously perfect sacrifice from Heaven that began right there—right then—a sacrifice that changed the world and echoes down through the generations with a miraculous song of sweet salvation, perfect love, and wonderful, flowing grace.

She put down her wine glass and walked over to the ever green symbol of ever lasting life beautifully adorned and brightly lit, and dropping to her knees she began to cry. The tears were those of joy and thankfulness. She remained there for a while, in sweet conversation with her Savior and as she openly and sincerely shared her heart with Him, she asked Him to send His Angels to watch over her mate, wherever he is, whoever he is and to please keep him safe in His hands. She thanked Him for His faithfulness, and for always hearing her prayers. As she rose from the floor she wiped her tears, took a deep breath and settled back to enjoy the peacefulness that filled the room. She was thankful that she had decided to have a date with Jesus on Christmas Eve....a sweetly blessed birthday party of the noteworthy, spiritual kind with gifts that are ....ageless and timeless...and wonderfully everlasting.

Chapter 7

Patrick loved Christmas Eve. He usually spent it with Kelly and Ana, and their families at the Café, which was always closed to the public from Christmas Eve until after the New Year. It was a commitment that Kelly and Ana made to each other…a festive time of rest, celebration, and a break from their busy schedules to enjoy family, friends and refreshment.

The café had been lively with Christmas music, a smorgasbord of holiday delights and plenty of *Yuletide Spirit*. In the midst of the evening, keeping with tradition, Kelly and Ana called for a quiet moment of prayer, and everybody gathered in a circle, joining hands and taking turns going around the affectionate sphere of holiday cheer with their own personal contributions, in love and thanksgiving.

After the prayer, Kelly and Ana surprisingly announced to

the gathering of familiar, loving faces that they were not only pregnant with the joys of the season, but they were also pregnant with child.... to the delight of everyone present, and would be welcoming their first perfect little son or daughter into the circle by late spring. The entire crowd rang out with thunderous applause and congratulations were abundantly delivered.

After the celebration concluded, and lots of hugs and well wishes, Patrick made his way home. With his end of year, busy schedule he hadn't had much time for seasonal decorating. At the last minute he bought a little two-foot tall artificial tree that came already decorated with little twinkle lights, bows and tiny ornaments, just to liven up the house with some resemblance of Christmas and placed it on the window table next to the manger scene that his mother had affectionately passed down to him many years before.

It was finally quiet—all the music, singing, and laughter was now a fading memory and he found his thoughts once again drawn back to Kandi....wondering how she was spending her Christmas Eve. As he pondered the time difference, he concluded that she was more than likely asleep by then and laughed as he silently hoped those visions of sugar plums dancing in her head would be softly whispering his name as they hopped about her psyche in holiday cheer.

He glanced over to the table that showcased his meagerly decorative expression of Christmas and took notice of the star on top of the manger. Stars always reminded him of fated events and destiny—that magical moment when the so called cosmic-tumblers would supernaturally and perfectly fall into place and the great big expansive universe would spaciously open up broad and wide to show you what is beautifully and miraculously possible.

He turned to the spectacularly lit sky outside of the window where he discovered once again the most magnificent Christmas light display amazingly suspended high above the Earth—reminding him of the awesomeness of God and filling him with the desire and need to pray. He prayed for his sister Caroline and her dear family. He prayed for Kelly and Ana, and thanked God for the blessing of their beautiful friendship and asked His special blessing upon their unborn child—and then he prayed for Kandi. The twilight in the road up ahead kept him from seeing clearly, and he sincerely asked God to shine His light upon the pathway that would lead him safely and directly back to her.

What he could see clearly was Kandi Kayne—how enchanting she was—and how perfectly appealing she was to every sense and sensibility he had. He remembered feeling so incredibly relaxed and free sitting there with her as if any emotional walls he had constructed upon his pathway until that point in time were falling apart into a pile of rubble at his feet and disappearing into nothingness as if they never even existed in the first place. She made him feel validated, as if finally somebody out there heard the deepest meanderings of his soul and resounded with a loud, "YES! I hear you—my heart feels what your heart feels—my soul resonates on the same frequency.........

I TOTALLY GET YOU!" She caused such an adrenalin rush inside him as if he'd just awakened from a very long sleep and found himself in a strange and beautiful paradise...a place his heart had yearned for long before he ever found himself there.

He was positively amazed at how she could open him up—like the gush of a waterfall cascading down the side of a majestic mountaintop and spilling over….into the landscape as if nothing could prevent it from taking its proper place in the midst of her.

It was like discovering a new island, lush with beauty, fragrance and delectable delights, realizing it was actually his—had been there all along and all he had to do was open up his eyes and give himself permission to truly see it.

He found himself wishing that they were someplace wonderful together, seeing the sights, hearing the sounds, experiencing the smells and tastes of Christmas which he somehow knew would be experienced completely different in her presence.

He felt as if he had received an early Christmas present…a magical, mystical, surprisingly wonderful gift that awakened his heart and soul to all that life suddenly held possible for him.

He was wishing that some brilliant Quantum Physicist had really built that "time machine" because he decided without a doubt that he would be the first one to volunteer to be strapped in and carried back to his future…. Right there in the little airport café where he would most definitely not make the same mistake twice of allowing her to vanish from sight without at least getting her number before she dashed off. If he could somehow magically rewind the whole scenario and begin again, he would have been quite careful to tell her how much he wanted to see her again, and would have never allowed her to leave without some kind of purposeful plan in place to put them back together again in the near future. "Oh the sweet wisdom and revelation of hindsight," he thought.

He realized that even though they may never pass that way again it seemed as if the universe had whispered sweet secrets into his spirit about the future, and filled him with hopes that he would be sharing that future with her. He had come to a definite determination that in the New Year he would be making it a priority to locate her if he had to search to the ends of the Earth and back. The New Year was the beginning of a new mission, and his *Christmas Wish* was for his entire life to be filled with the delightful taste of Kandi Kayne.

And with that settled, Patrick relaxed into his chair where sweet thoughts and lovely dreams of sunny days, starry nights, and lazy afternoons spent with her, touching each other in the deepest of places, filled up all the dreamy spaces of his mind and made that Christmas Eve the most magical one he could ever remember.

Chapter 8

As the misty days of winter faded into spring, Kandi was happy to accept Stacy's invitation to join her and Chris for a little off shore sailing weekend. The weather was perfectly wonderful, the seas were going to be calm with a steady breeze and she was ready to pack a bag and get out on those refreshing open seas after what seemed like a relatively long winter. "Nothing like the good ole, fresh salt air to clean the cobwebs out of your psyche," she thought.

Her career was going very well and she found herself quite thankful for the fact that she had been so busy, as it kept her mind off of the loneliness she felt. She had pretty much given up hope of ever hearing from Patrick Calahan again, figuring if he hadn't called in all that time he definitely wasn't interested.

She found it rather frustrating as she was usually very intuitively perceptive and she strongly felt his interest in her. She couldn't help but wonder how she could have been so incredibly wrong about that one.

"Oh well, so much for that," she stated, as she picked up her bag and headed out the door. She walked over to Stacy's house and through the back yard to the boat that was securely tied in their slip, where she tossed in her overnight bag and headed back to her car.

She decided to make a quick little trip to the winery for several bottles of her favorite wine to take along for the weekend. It was just a short drive from Topsail Island to her favorite winery and it was well worth the trip as far as she was concerned. She made her way through the lovely little gift shop and noticed a large group of people doing a wine tasting at the bar. She was sorry she didn't have time to sit down and join them as she dearly loved trying out all of their newest wines, and having lunch in their lovely Bistro was always a special treat.

She couldn't help but stop to look around the gift shop with all of its unique and special little items. Her favorite part was the section of wine stoppers. One of them caught her eye immediately and brought her to a screeching halt. It was a little Santa Claus with two little dangling legs and feet that would comically hang down over the side of the wine bottle when the stopper was in place. She couldn't resist, and quickly placed it in her basket as she laughed.

She purchased several bottles of her favorite wine along with several bottles as a gift for Stacy and Chris for inviting her along and quickly made her way back to Topsail Island. As she pulled in the driveway she was greeted excitedly by Stacy and Chris as they bounced down their deck steps to load the boat with supplies for their weekend outing.

They were all quite excited at the prospect of getting away for the weekend. Within the half hour they were motoring their way along the sound anxiously heading toward the inlet. As they rounded the first buoy they opened up the sails followed by a few moments of peaceful silence as the experience always left them breathless for a while. After a few moments, Stacy shouted out a "whooooohoooooo" into the wind, and they all smiled and drew in a deep breath as they magnificently made their way out into the open waters of the beautiful blue Atlantic.

The day was perfectly wonderful as they tacked along the coastline with gloriously majestic dolphins happily leaping, and energetically playing at their bow. It always seemed like a gift from Heaven when they would show up to follow the boat. They seemed to bring extraordinary messages of love whispered in the winds and waves as if they are privy to ageless, spiritual information that is beyond human understanding and revelation and they come to whisper them softly into the spirits of those cast upon the waters of the sea. They leave a lasting impression that never fades in the shifting sands of the passage of time.

Shortly after sunset in the perfectly dreamy twilight they made their way back to the sound, and threw out the anchors for the night. Stacy had gone to the grocery store and bought three incredible filets to cook on the gas grill that hung on the starboard side rail—it was a gift from Kandi the previous Christmas and they were quite anxious to try it out. Kandi placed foiled potatoes previously baked and stuffed with scallions, cheese and bacon on the grill to be reheated while the steaks were marinating and they opened a chilled bottle of wine and turned on some soft jazz as the evening breeze caressed the landscape with a fresh touch of soothing salt air.

At that point it was hard to imagine that anything could be better but Kandi was really feeling the empty space beside her as she looked at Stacy and Chris sitting across from her on the aft deck lovingly wrapped around each other and the empty space beside her grew bigger and wider as she felt the emptiness closing in.

She quickly gathered herself and with wine in hand made her way to the bow, flopping comfortably down to enjoy the glorious view and deciding to give her dear friends some time to be alone together on such a delightfully beautiful evening on the water.

Dinner was amazingly enjoyable, the company was perfect and the atmosphere was breathtaking. After clearing away the mess, they took turns for a brief shower and sat back under the brightly shining stars to enjoy the wonder of the beautifully painted portrait before them.

A little while later Stacy and Chris went off to bed, and Kandi poured the last bit of wine out of the bottle, pulling a cover up over her. As she leaned back to nestle in a pillow behind her back..... she looked up to capture the starry night sky. She couldn't remember a lovelier night on the water. The sky was amazing and completely peppered with heavenly lights. As she gazed into the expanse of space above her, she couldn't help but feel the awesome presence of God. Suddenly her space beside her didn't feel so empty after all.

He had a way of filling up all her empty spaces when she would stop long enough to be mindful of Him and invite Him there. She loved coming to the quiet to be with Him, and knew that He understood the cries of her soul, and the longings of her heart. She could share all of them with Him easily, and cast her cares upon Him, knowing that He truly cared for her. She began to tell him of her loneliness, and her desire for a mate. Not just any mate, but *THE* mate....the one that HE had lovingly prepared for her all of his life. The one that would dot her I's and perfectly complete her life sentence....the one that holds her destiny in his heart and soul. As she began talking about him, a tear found its way down her cheek as she could almost touch him, he felt so close at that moment.

As she imagined him there beside her, along with the gentle rocking of the water, she found herself completely relaxed, and within a few moments she fell asleep. In the midst of her starry sleep she had a dream....she was moving along the waters in the boat quite swiftly in her dream, and as if dancing upon the soft and gentle whispers of the evening breeze, she heard a soft, comforting voice say, "Write him a letter and share your heart and soul with him. Ask him to meet you at your favorite Italian café in St. Augustine next Christmas Eve, and wait for him there. Cast your letter upon the sea with a simple prayer of faith and allow Me to put My Personal stamp on it for delivery."

She awakened with a startle and for a moment she questioned what had just happened, but somewhere deep inside she knew she had received a *Divine message* of instruction, and she was immediately determined to follow it to the letter.

She reached for her bag, quickly grabbed her journal and pen, and sat back waiting for the words to begin. She felt an adrenalin rush as the words began to come like subtle messages delivered from another realm of space and time. They began to flow like the tides destined to make their way back out to sea.

"My Beloved, I have waited all my life for you. Somehow I know that in the midst of this writing there is a sacred stamp of blessing that will deliver my love letter right into your hands. I know that no other will ever be able to find this message, as it is written just for you...only for you. I believe our stars are destined to cross at the perfect time. I ask you to reach out and catch the star that forever twinkles inside your heart and it will lead you to your destiny's path....follow that pathway and uncover the sweet sunrises that await you there. Take hold of this precious opportunity along with me while it brightly sparkles before us.

I have always believed that my greatest goals are attainable as long as I commit myself to them, and I commit myself to you, right now. Though roadblocks may have stood in the way of our dreams and desires to find each other for a time, we must remember that our very destiny is hiding right now behind those barriers and it is the seemingly broken roads that have led us to each other at this moment, as you are standing there holding this letter in your hands. The delays we faced while getting here were simple stepping stones to our dreams-come-true.

I deeply value you, my love, along with all of your wonderful capabilities, characteristics and talents for they are what make you uniquely you...the one God created just for me.

The greatest gifts in life are not purchased but are acquired by prayer, faith and determination. I have prayed for you, I have faith in you and I am determined to spend my life with you. Your song sings softly and sweetly inside my heart and I know if I forget the words to mine you are the only one on earth who can patiently and lovingly help me to remember them.

Meet me at Scaletta's Italian Café in St. Augustine, Florida on Christmas Eve at noon for Christmas tea. I'll be waiting there for you, my precious love. Bring the bottle in which you found this letter with you so I will recognize you when you come in the door. You'll see me sitting there at the table by the window in a red dress. I'll see you there, my beloved. Thank you for giving OUR hopes and dreams everything you've got and never giving up on me....you will catch the shooting star that holds your destiny, I promise.

All my heart......"

She took a deep breath and tore the pages from her journal, folding them and placing them in her bag. She washed the beautiful cobalt blue wine bottle out thoroughly and wrapped it in her towel to dry. She thanked God for keeping the message of her heart in safe keeping, and for miraculously delivering it into the hands of her soul mate. As she looked at the tide tables she realized that the following day would be the perfect time to cast her message out to sea as the tides would be rushing out in the early afternoon as they would be off shore sailing. She decided to wait until then to mail her letter.

She quickly and peacefully settled into her comfortable bunk filled with joy, faith and anticipation for the following day. It was a beautifully calm night with soothing, gentle rocking that lovingly escorted her into a sweet sleep.

As the new beginnings of the risen Sun ushered in a glorious new day, she bounced out of bed with excitement at the joys that lie ahead. She couldn't possibly hide her enthusiasm to get under way. Stacy jokingly asked, "What kind of star dust fell on you last night as you polished off that bottle of wine, I could use some of that stuff this morning, myself!" And Chris quickly chimed in, "Me too!"

After a cup of coffee and some bagels with cream cheese, they were finally under way and before long they were back out over the open sea enjoying another fabulously picturesque day.

With the boat on auto-pilot Stacy and Chris went up on the bow to relax with their feet dangling over the side, enjoying the sea breeze on their faces and the beauty of the day.

While she smiled as she observed them, and was so thankful for the fact that her dear friend Stacy found her perfect mate, Kandi realized it was time to launch her letter. She removed it from her bag and neatly placed it in the bottle. As she was about to put the cork in the bottle, she remembered the little Santa Claus bottle stopper, wondering if it would be able to withstand the trip, and then she giggled to herself, "Of course it will…if this message can be *Divinely* delivered to my soul mate, that stopper can make it along for the trip!" She quickly retrieved it from her little bag and placed it tightly in the bottle with the cork deeply recessed inside. With a soft prayer she tossed it into the sea, and before the bottle even hit the water a family of dolphins popped up all around the stern of the boat. Within a matter of seconds she watched as one of them grabbed her bottle and they disappeared into the depths.

She was stunned and truly amazed as she realized that God was using them to deliver her letter. Obviously the tides needed a little help to carry it to the right place at the right time and she was thrilled to know in her heart and soul that her letter was miraculously on its way into the hands of the only one *Divinely* destined to receive it.

Chapter 9

The lazy days of summer had finally arrived and Patrick was looking forward to getting away from his everyday surroundings to vacation with his dearest friends, Kelly, and Ana and their families. They gathered together at the seashore in the Outer Banks of North Carolina every year at mid-summer and rented a huge monstrosity of a beach house for the entire week of sun, fun, and total relaxation. Patrick felt like such a part of the family and was always delighted to be involved in the plans.

The winter and spring months had kept him quite busy with work as well as the determined efforts of a vigorous attempt to find his missing link to no avail.

"Project Candy Cane" was still ongoing, and he was zealously fighting the beginning pangs of discouragement. With the phone at her home on Topsail Island still listed

under her parent's name, something she'd been meaning to change and never got around to—it was virtually impossible to find her through a phone listing. He had exhausted many attempts to locate her and was beginning to wonder if the whole encounter that day in the airport café was something he dreamed or imagined and hadn't really happened at all. He was happy for the vacation break, as he needed to get his mind on some relaxation for a while that would hopefully renew his spirit and refresh his faith in the future.

His bags were packed for the week and he was waiting for the call from Kelly to leave for the airport. With the new little baby girl in the house they had lots of extra packing to do to get ready for the trip. Patrick was thrilled to be a God-father to the lovely little Brianna, and was looking quite forward to experiencing more of her during the week. It was wonderful to see the happiness that she brought to her family and Patrick found himself longing for one sweet day when he would be able to look down into the angelic face of his own firstborn wrapped in the arms of a loving and beautiful mother whom he adored, and be able to experience it first hand. "I am so incredibly ready for that in my life," he thought.

The phone rang suddenly and jarred him right out of his thoughts to quickly answer it.

"This is your airport escort service, Mr. Calahan, ready to whisk you off for a week of ridiculous pleasure, pathetically disgusting overindulgence, positively sinful excess and down right gluttony! Are you ready to go, Sir?"

It's about time you got here, you slovenly disgusting, and

nauseating slacker, I almost had to wait!" He said, as he heard a loud belly laugh echoing through the phone. "Be right there, Buddy."

He grabbed his bags and practically left skid marks out the door to gratefully reach the vehicle of escape, and shortly thereafter they were on their way to the airport.

The flight was relatively uneventful and in a few short hours they were checking into the beach house, and getting settled in for the week. Ana's sister, and her husband and children were with them, as well as Kelly's brother and his family. The house was positively filled with the excitement of a happy family on vacation, and the energy was more than incredible. They always drew straws to see how the bedrooms would be distributed among them, and soon Patrick was unpacking his suitcase and relaxing across the bed for a brief moment of repose.

The day went by rather quickly and before long they were sitting out on the deck after dinner in rocking chairs that lined the porch enjoying the sight of a moon waxing full and shining brightly, leaving a lighted, glistening pathway across the water. It was like the ever so sweet icing on the simply delicious cake having a full moon to enjoy while they were there.

The days that followed were filled with wonderful laughter, an abundance of joy, fine entertainment, great seafood, and very good company. There was only one big problem....it was always rather amazing how rapidly and swiftly the week always flew by, and before they knew it the last day was quickly upon them.

Patrick rose very early with an urgent desire to catch the morning sunrise. The house was quiet and everyone was fast asleep, so he gently closed the door behind him and walked softly down the stairs to the beach. He spread a towel out and sat down to wait, and before long he found himself taking in the splendor of the most magnificent portrait, painted in real-time, and spread forth like a magical, mystical tapestry to perfectly and completely delight the senses.

As the glorious Sun made its ascent over the horizon he noticed a family of dolphins just out beyond the breakers and watched them curiously. They were fascinating creatures that absolutely mesmerized him. It was always a delight to see them frolicking about in the pristine waters of the Atlantic, and it was certainly a great way to begin a new day.

Suddenly he caught sight of an object bouncing and rolling in the surf. The early morning Sun provided just enough light to plainly see it was making its way to shore. He quickly jumped from his towel and with an anticipatory jog, he made his way to the waters edge to find it securely wedged in the sand beneath him. The excitement began to build as he bent over and noticed there was a note inside, and an incredibly comical Santa Claus cork secured tightly in the top of the mysterious blue bottle. He quickly picked it up, and carefully carried it back to his towel to wipe it off. After he thoroughly dried the bottle he reached for the cork and eagerly removed it, reaching passionately for the mystifying contents. As he removed the note, he carefully unfolded it and quite curiously began to read.

He could feel his heart begin to race as he ardently made his way down the note to take in the beautiful words so lovingly poured out upon the page. His mind was soaring as he devoured each line like a starving man having his first meal in a very long time. The words she wrote touched him in sacred places that had never been reached before. He didn't even know those places existed until that very moment in time. As he reached the last paragraph, he could hardly catch his breath from the exhilaration he felt deep inside. It was like having an answered prayer magically delivered in a most amazing and surprising way, and suddenly a whole new screen was visible to finally view what felt like the beginnings of a dream-come-true.

He sat motionless for a long time staring out into the sea, trying to take it in—to absorb the new information that seemed to light up his brain like an electric shockwave.

"This couldn't just be a coincidence," he thought. In his years of study he had come to understand that there was no such thing. This really was happening…and it was happening to him, right there…right then. Of all the people who could have found that message, it came to him and no one else. Everything inside him cried out, "Pay close attention—this is vitally important."

He read the note again, and again, and again. Each time he read it, the emotions grew stronger and stronger as if the message inside that bottle was written and perfectly recognized by his very own soul from the ageless, timeless past and was finding its way to him at that magical and fated moment in time as part of a predestined plan established long before he drew his first breath. The person who wrote that note felt strangely and outlandishly familiar—clearly recognizable by every part of his senses.

"No wonder I was never able to find my mystery date from the airport café. My destiny was leading me to this place and time and all the events of my life are unfolding just as they are meant to do," he thought. "Oh how on earth am I going to make it until Christmas Eve," he wondered, " and to be invited to *Christmas Tea*, for only the second time in my life......oh it couldn't be her, it just couldn't be her, could it?"

Abruptly he heard a voice calling out, "Hey Beach Bum, get your lazy carcass up here and join us, we're going out for some breakfast." Kelly's familiar voice brought a chuckle and Patrick immediately decided to wrap the bottle into his towel to avoid any questions or explanations. He was definitely not ready to talk about this latest development just yet. He hadn't had time to even thoroughly absorb it himself, or know quite what to do with all the feelings and emotions it deeply stirred within him.

As they sat across from each other at the breakfast house Kelly smiled at Patrick and said, "Hmmmmm, that sunrise this morning seems to have plugged you into some pretty positive energy. I haven't seen you like this since you returned from your little candy cane adventure last Christmas, there Buddy."

"Oh it's amazing what a morning sunrise can do for ya," he replied, knowing that Kelly always seemed to pick up even the most subtle differences in his emotional landscape, and would more than likely press him to fess up sooner or later. But for now, later was better and he continued enjoying the amazing bounty before him holding his secret safe within the carefully hidden recesses of his mind.

Life as he knew it had taken a significant turn that morning, and he completely and wholeheartedly understood that. "Is it Christmas yet?" He laughed to himself.

Chapter 10

K andi struggled down the attic steps with the holiday decorations quite eager to dress the house all up in Christmas once again. It had certainly been a long wait, and she decided even though she would be spending Christmas in St. Augustine, she still wanted to enjoy the wonderful *Yuletide Spirit* that always accompanied the decorating. Skimping on Christmas was simply not her style at all.

Her parents had planned a trip to Italy for Christmas, and normally she would have been elated to accept their invitation to join them, but this year she had a very important date to keep that she wasn't about to miss for any reason— even Christmas in Tuscany!

She was excited to be visiting her Aunt Grace for Christmas. She was always such a delight. It was her mother's sister who apparently had taken a lovely swim in the very same Christmas gene pool, as she was just as much a Christmas nut as her mother had always been. Christmas was always much more fun spending it with people who have an exceptional love for the special holiday. They make it much more spectacular.

It was visiting her Aunt Grace that led Kandi and Stacy to their favorite little Italian café quite a few years before that long since remained at the very tip top of their A-list. She was so looking forward to visiting the place again, especially with such a special *Christmas Tea* date awaiting her.

The weeks after Thanksgiving sailed by swiftly, wrapped all up in holiday cheer, with parties, shopping, baking, wrapping, and all the tremendously happy experiences that come with the joys of the season.

The time had come where she found herself in the midst of packing for her trip.

She went to the closet and removed the beautiful dress she had bought for her special occasion to admire it a little before placing it in the garment bag. It was a deep scarlet red which was always one of her favorites and she wore it beautifully with the princess waste that flattered her lovely figure quite nicely.

She tried to imagine herself there and quickly the butterflies filled her tummy with excitement. She had battled the doubts and fears for quite a while since that magical weekend out on the sea. Lingering little doubts still tried to taunt her with notions that she was only setting herself up for a great big disappointing let down, but she always managed to find her way back to her faith. She finally decided to shelf those remaining little doubts once and for all, and open her heart to thankfully receive whatever was coming with gratitude and appreciation. "Whatever will be—will be," she thought, "and my intention is to expect the miraculous and simply sit back and wait with great expectation for it to show up."

Several days before Christmas Eve she got together with Stacy and Chris to exchange novelty Christmas presents over a delightful dinner and enjoyable evening. Stacy could hardly contain her excitement when Kandi finally confessed to her the events that took place that weekend out on the sailboat. She pleaded with Kandi to promise that she would call her as soon as she possibly could to give her the complete details of her fated *Christmas Tea Party*, and Kandi agreed as they tried to imagine together that magical moment when he would walk through the door of their favorite café.

The following morning she loaded her car with goodies to take to her Aunt Grace, pulled happily out of the driveway and began her journey to St. Augustine. She always enjoyed a car trip during the Christmas season, cranking up the holiday tunes way beyond high, and singing her heart out all the way to her destination.

Her Aunt Grace was so very happy to see her, and Kandi spent the entire day before Christmas Eve catching her up and recounting the events of her experience that weekend on the boat.

Her aunt was thrilled to see Kandi following the dreams of her heart—determined to continuously muster the courage

60

to follow them all the way to the end. She encouraged her to always remain open to the wonderful things life brings along, fully expecting that all will be well. "It is in your prayer of faith that your miracles are born, but it is in your unwavering expectation that the miracles find their powerful place of manifestation in the midst of your reality," she reminded her.

Kandi absolutely loved talking with her Aunt Grace. She seemed to be plugged into a powerfully infinite light source that instilled her with the wisdom of the ages and the ability to share it so easily with others. It was always inspiring to be with her, and especially before such an important meeting. Kandi could clearly see why the *Heavenly Voice* in the message steered her to this place for such a meeting. Her Aunt Grace would help her prepare her mind and heart for the miraculous event, and it was becoming more and more clear that all was just as it should be and moving along perfectly as planned.

Patrick was ecstatic as his eyes caught a glance of the calendar on his desk and he enthusiastically began counting down the days. It seemed like an eternity waiting for Christmas to arrive. Although his life had been full and busy since that astonishing mid-summer's day on the beach, each and every day since that fated day his predominant thought process was focused ardently on his trip to St. Augustine for Christmas. It was quite amazing how well the whole thing worked out because he had promised to spend Christmas with his sister Caroline and her family.

They lived in a little town called Yulee, just outside of Jacksonville, so a drive to St. Augustine would be a piece of cake from there. It had been three years since he spent a Christmas with them and he was looking forward to catching up with his sister and her dear family. But, that was not the most important thing on his mind.

He had wrestled with many reservations about the whole situation through the months that followed that day on the beach. He knew how perfectly absurd and ridiculous it sounded, and he wasn't surprised at all when he witnessed the sincere look of concern on his best friend's face when he told him of his plans and the events that led him to them. He knew that Kelly loved him like a brother, and it was only out of love, care and concern that he was skeptical of the uncertain road ahead for his friend. But, once Patrick had a chance to really share his deepest feelings and emotions that he experienced, and allowed him to read the letter that arrived so miraculously that day, even dubious Kelly was thoroughly convinced there was a greater mind present in this unlikely situation, and agreed that Patrick should follow it through.

Kelly once again ushered Patrick to the airport, and hugged him goodbye with a loud *"Merry Christmas"* shout as he watched him disappear beyond the security section.

A few anxious hours later, he was pulling into his sister's driveway with his rental car and fervently ringing the door bell. He immediately heard footsteps and giggles running to the door and he could feel the excitement building as the door opened to reveal a group of loving, smiling and eager faces that he held so close to his heart.

After a wonderful evening of family time, the children were off to bed, and Patrick was able to sit down with his sister and catch up with all the events of her life since they'd been together last. His brother-in-law insisted on cleaning up the dinner mess to Caroline's delight, and Patrick's surprise. She poured them a cup of fresh coffee and sat back to thoroughly enjoy some special time with her brother.

It was not at all a surprise that it took her no time at all to begin to interrogate him about his social life—specifically wanting to know if there was somebody special.....*YET.*

He laughed and assured her that somebody very special had indeed come into his life. He just hadn't met her yet! "What do you mean you haven't met her yet, my bro? What kind of answer is that? She demanded. With that Patrick began his story and by the time he got around to letting her read the note, she had a stream of tears rolling down her face.

"I have never read anything so beautiful in my life," she stated, matter-of-factly.

"My goodness, I can hardly wait to meet this woman myself! But, Patrick, how do you know this letter is not very old, and that this meeting was supposed to take place long ago? Did you ever consider that?" She asked.

"Oh, trust me, Caroline, I considered a lot of things, and I tossed around different doubts and fears for quite some time, but I can only tell you how I FEEL. What I may think is irrelevant at this point. It's what I feel that keeps me perpetually moving toward this fateful meeting. And like you, I am thoroughly convinced that the woman who wrote this letter has the most beautiful heart and soul I have ever encountered and I have to follow this path and find out what lies at the end of this magnificently beautiful rainbow, because turning back now goes against everything I feel in my heart and soul. So, it's all systems GO, and prepare to launch," he finished.

Chapter 11

K andi was thrilled to finally wake up to Christmas Eve—a very special Christmas Eve indeed, and she had anxiously awaited its arrival.

Her Aunt Grace knocked once lightly on the bedroom door and opened it, carrying a tray of breakfast goodies, and delivering a boisterous *"Morning Glory"* as she happily placed the delightful tray upon the nightstand beside the bed.

The house smelled incredibly of freshly brewed coffee and something wonderfully sweet that made Kandi's mouth begin to water with anticipation.

"What's that wonderful aroma sweetly filling the house, My Dear Aunt Grace?"

"It's my homemade spice-coffee cake, My Dear—and freshly squeezed Florida orange juice," she proudly replied. "Oh, Aunt Grace, it smells and looks perfectly divine."

"Well, this is a *Divinely ordained* day and I feel you should start it out with a perfectly peaceful breakfast in bed. You have a very big day ahead. You should spend some quiet time with God while you eat, and then we must begin the preparations for getting you ready, My Dear." " Getting me ready?" Kandi asked inquisitively. "Of course Dear, you must first relax in a hot bubbly bath, and then we must give you a little mini-manicure and pedicure, of course—and then we must urgently dote on your hair, making sure that every shiny, beautiful strand is curled to absolute perfection in flawlessly dangling tresses down the back of your lovely scarlet red dress. We'll fuss a bit over your make-up, spray you with your best perfume, and send you on your way to your favorite little restaurant where your *Heavenly inspired destiny* awaits you," she finished. "Aunt Grace, you are an Angel and just so much fun!" She affectionately replied. "Well, I am certainly not an Angel, Dear, but I'm sure I've entertained a few in my day and probably kept at least one quite busy keeping me out of trouble," she laughed.

With that, she hurried from the room and softly closed the door behind her leaving Kandi to her breakfast—her thoughts—and her God.

As Kandi reached for her coffee, she stopped and decided to have some prayer time before she enjoyed her lovingly prepared Christmas Eve morning delights.

*"Heavenly Father, I hardly even know where to begin. I guess **I love you with all my heart and all my soul** would probably be a good place to start. I am so thankful and positively filled with infinite love and gratitude for Your tender, loving care. I know that You faithfully watch over me every minute of every day and have since before I took in my first earthly breath. Thank You! Thank You that YOUR WORD is forever established in Heaven and on Earth. Thank You for Your WORD MADE FLESH—Jesus and His incredible Christmas gift that by His stripes I am perfectly healed, delivered, and washed whiter than snow. Thank You for all my dear family and friends—bless them Father. And, I thank You for your faithfulness in delivering my soul mate. Whatever his name, his background, his profession—I know he is blessed by You and perfectly made just for me. Thank You from the deepest part of my heart for the miracle I am about to encounter. You have my word that I will work tirelessly on myself through all our days together to be the best helpmate, companion, exhorter and friend he could possibly have. I will love him with all my heart—all the days of my life. And, through the years as the fire starts to mellow and the pages of our love story begin to yellow with age—I will love him just the same, and try to give him a glimpse of YOU in everything I do. Please send your Angels to go before me and prepare the way ahead. I trust you, and believe this will be the best cup of Christmas Tea I've ever had! In perfect faith, I pray. Amen."*

After enjoying the lovely breakfast the preparations began. Kandi could hardly remember when she ever felt quite so pampered. She felt like a princess being prepared to meet her handsome prince who would finally ride up on his magnificent white stallion and carry her away to happiness-ever after.

After several hours of fun-filled primping and fussing, she took one last glance into the mirror, and laughed as she said, "Mirror, mirror on the wall, I am going to meet my destiny and together we're going to create the most beautiful reflection of all." Her Aunt Grace chuckled with her, and stood back gazing at her with the look of unconditional love and absolute approval. "You look incredibly lovely, My Dear! Now go—with the blessings of Heaven and the Angels who stand in the presence of God to escort you all along the way." She walked her to the door, and with a warm hug wished her well as Kandi walked out to the driveway looking more beautiful than she had ever looked before.

The drive to Scaletta's Restaurant was an anxious one and she was happy to arrive a little early to have some time to settle her nerves a bit before the clock struck that long anticipated noon hour.

She was graciously greeted as she entered and quickly escorted to her reserved table near the front window. As she looked around the restaurant to all the lovely Christmas decorations she glanced to the window and to her surprise, recognized the decorative holly garland that graced the lovely glass panes as it swiftly triggered the memory of the dream she had the night she returned from her encounter with Patrick Calahan that day in the airport café. Her eyes took a quick sweep all around the restaurant as the dream began to emerge into full consciousness and she felt as if she was reliving it at that very moment.

" Oh, it couldn't be him, that's ridiculous, I was just filled with thoughts of him that night and that is why he showed up so vividly in my dreams—and of course this is my favorite place so why wouldn't my subconscious mind place us here?" She thought. And with that she quickly dismissed it. The little butterflies were making themselves known more and more as each minute ticked by and she sat back as comfortably as she could to continue the wait......five minutes and counting.......

Patrick was awakened by the first morning light coming into the guest room where he slept, and almost immediately smiled, realizing the day was finally here.

He took a deep breath and blew it out slowly trying hard to dismiss those little doubts and fears that seemed determined to creep into his mind. "I am not going to allow anything to ruin this long awaited day," he thought.

He quickly pulled on his pants and sweatshirt and headed for the kitchen where the wonderfully inviting aroma of fresh coffee called out to him loudly, and he found Caroline there at the kitchen table reading the local newspaper in the quiet peacefulness of the early morning as the children and her husband still slept.

"Good Morning, Brother Dear, and Merry Christmas. Help yourself to some coffee—it's a fresh pot," she lovingly stated. "Thank you my kindly sister, I don't mind if I do, and besides that, you always make the best coffee," he declared with a warm smile.

"Patrick, whatever happens today, I want you to know that

I love you, and I am right here to support you, no matter what!" She stated firmly. "Well, although that strongly hints of skepticism, I will graciously say *thank you* anyway," he replied with a big grin and sat back to enjoy his coffee.

Before long, he was showered, dressed and a bit nervously headed out the door. He paused in the car and prayed for a while before pulling out of the driveway and began his little journey to St. Augustine where he was determined to indeed catch that shooting star that held his destiny—as promised. He stopped along the way and purchased a beautiful red rose which he placed perfectly in the cobalt blue wine bottle that had so phenomenally delivered his fated message on that amazing mid-summer day.

The drive was quite peaceful with Christmas music softly playing on the car stereo. In what seemed like a relatively short time he had arrived in St. Augustine. After a few wrong turns he found Scaletta's Restaurant and quite nervously pulled into an extraordinarily convenient parking space not too far from the front door which seemed to have been remarkably reserved just for him. As he nervously prepared to open the car door his pulse began to increase significantly and the adrenalin poured through his system like a raging river cresting its banks. "Okay, it's show time!" He thought, and reached for the door handle.

As he stepped onto the sidewalk he glanced to the creatively decorated entrance to the front door of Scaletta's restaurant, and quite suddenly began to see vibrant flashes of the dream he'd had the night after his unexpected encounter with Kandi Kayne. He felt a surge of energy when he began to recognize the street, the building, even the Christmas decorations looked strangely familiar. As his eyes caught sight of the water fountain outside he remembered seeing it clearly ....it was unmistakably the same one and this was no doubt the same place he saw that night vividly in his dream... with that realization, and bottle in hand he unconsciously began to run.....

Kandi tensely peeked at her watch and caught sight of the second hand brushing softly across the twelve to usher in the noon hour right on schedule. As she turned to look out the window her heart seemed to jump in her throat as she noticed the figure of a man running to the front door of the restaurant carrying the familiar bottle that she knew so well. As the door flew open wide it was as if the entire building and everyone in it completely disappeared at that very moment and standing there with his heart pounding wildly, was Patrick Calahan in all his glory, proudly holding up the bottle like a prized trophy. He took one look at her and shouted, *"OH MY GOD... MISS KAYNE....it's YOU! It's YOU! OH MY GOD, It's really YOU!"*

As she stood to her feet trembling all over she could hardly believe the miracle before her and responded with a loud, *"YES, Mr. Calahan, thank God it's YOU! I wanted it so badly to be you!"* He hurriedly sat the bottle on the table to reach for her and she quickly opened her arms to welcome him closer for a sweet, loving, and long awaited embrace.

He pulled back to look deeply into her eyes as if to gently open the windows of their souls to formally invite each other in...before his lips enthusiastically found hers in a sweet, lovely kiss. As they reluctantly parted to look at each other again they both burst into laughter as the incredible events that led them there to that thrilling moment suddenly sank in.

He reached for the bottle with the beautiful red rose and lovingly handed it to her. "I believe this is for you, Kandi, and I think it's now safe and appropriate to say that you may call me Patrick," he laughed. "Yes, I dare say it is, and, you Sir may call me Mrs. Calahan!" She quickly replied, accompanied by a loud laugh, which caught him completely by surprise and perfectly delighted him at the same time.

"Yes Mam, there's no doubt about it.... as soon as I possibly can, in fact!" He laughingly and wholeheartedly agreed just as the waitress rounded the corner and placed before them their perfectly miraculous, destined and fated, long awaited cups of magical *Christmas Tea.*

Merry

Christmas

Merry Christmas
Candy Canes

Ingredients:

2 cups sugar
1/2 cup light corn syrup
1/2 cup water
1/4 teaspoon cream of tartar
3/4 teaspoon peppermint extract
Red food coloring

Preparation:

Cook sugar, corn syrup, water, and cream of tartar to a very hard ball stage (use candy thermometer: 250 to 265 degrees F.). Remove from heat and add peppermint. Divide into two parts and add red food coloring to one part and mix well.

Pull pieces of each part to form ropes and twist red around the white to make candy canes.

Yield: 1 dozen

Christmas Candy Cane Cocoa

Ingredients:

4 cups milk
3 ounces chocolate, chopped
4 red-and-white-striped peppermint candies, crushed
4 small red-and-white-striped candy canes
whipped cream

Directions:

1. In a saucepan bring the milk to a simmer.
2. Add the chocolate and the crushed peppermint candies and whisk until smooth.
3. Divide hot cocoa between four mugs garnish with whipped cream and serve with a candy cane stirring stick.

Makes 4 servings

Christmas Chocolate Candy Cane Brownies

Ingredients:

1 bar (4 oz) sweet baking chocolate
1/2 cup butter
2 eggs
1/4 cup sugar
2 teaspoons vanilla
1 cup flour
1/4 teaspoon salt
1/2 cup crushed candy canes
1/3 cup semisweet chocolate mini chips

Directions:

1. Preheat your oven to 350 degrees. Grease an 8 inch square pan and line the bottom with aluminum foil. Grease the aluminum foil and dust with flour (or cocoa).
2. In a small saucepan, melt the chocolate with butter over low heat.
3. In a large bowl, beat the eggs and sugar for 3 minutes on low speed.
4. Beat in the cooled chocolate mixture and vanilla extract.
5. Beat in the flour and salt until blended. Add the crushed peppermints and stir in the chocolate chips.

6. Pour into prepared pan.
7. Bake for 25 to 30 minutes. Cool.

Makes about 16 brownies.

Candy Cane Christmas Cheesecake

Ingredients:

1 cup chocolate wafer crumbs-
3 Tbsp margarine, melted
1 envelope unflavored gelatin
1/4 cup cold water
16 oz soft Philly cream cheese
1/2 cup sugar
1/2 cup milk
1/4 cup crushed candy canes
1 cup whipping cream, whipped
3 oz milk chocolate candy bars, chopped

Directions:

1. Combine wafer crumbs and margarine and press onto bottom of 9-inch spring-form pan. Bake at 350 degrees F. for 10 minutes. Cool.
2. Soften gelatin in water; stir over low heat until dissolved. Combine cream cheese and sugar, mixing at medium speed on electric mixer until well blended. Gradually add gelatin, milk and candy canes, mixing until blended, chill until slightly thickened but not set. Fold in whipped cream and chocolate.
3. Pour over crust. Chill until firm.
4. Garnish with additional whipped cream combined with crushed peppermint candies, if desired.

Candy Cane Christmas Fudge Pie

Ingredients:

24 chocolate cookies, crushed
1/2 cup butter or margarine
4 cups miniature marshmallows
1/2 cup milk
1 cup whipping cream
1/2 cup candy canes, crushed

Directions:

1. Combine cookies and melted butter or margarine. Press into 9 inch pie plate. Bake at 350 degrees F (175 degrees C) for 10 minutes. Cool.
2. Put 3 cups marshmallows in a double boiler. Add milk, and cook until
3. mixture melts and thickens. Cool in refrigerator for about 15 minutes.
4. In another bowl, whip the cream. Blend in the crushed candy canes and
5. remaining 1 cup marshmallows. Fold whipped cream mixture into melted
6. and cooled marshmallow mixture.
7. Pour into crust, and chill well before serving.

Makes 1 - 9 inch pie

Sharyn McIntyre

Candy Cane Christmas Snickerdoodles

Ingredients:

2 teaspoons ground cinnamon
1 1/2 cup sugar
1/2 cup butter, softened
1 teaspoon vanilla extract
2 eggs
2 cups flour
3/4 cup cocoa
1 teaspoon cream of tartar
1/2 teaspoon baking soda
1/4 teaspoon salt
2 tablespoons sugar
Red food coloring

Preparation:

Preheat oven to 400 degrees. Combine sugar, butter, vanilla and eggs; mix well. Stir in flour, cocoa, cream of tartar, baking soda and salt; blend well. Take half of mixture and place in separate bowl. Add 5 drops of red food coloring into one bowl and mix well. Shape 1 teaspoon dough from each half into a 4 inch rope. Place red and white ropes side by side; press together lightly and twist. Curve top of cookie down to form handle of candy cane. Combine 2 tablespoons sugar with 2 teaspoons ground cinnamon. Carefully dip candy canes into cinnamon mixture and cover with cinnamon. Place cookies on un-greased cookie sheet and bake 8-10 minutes or until set. Remove from cookie sheet immediately after removing from the oven. Place on cooling rack.

Options: You can alter the size of candy canes by using more or less dough. They're also amazingly good if you dip in Christmas sprinkles.

Sharyn McIntyre

Candy Cane Christmas Toffee

Ingredients

1 1/2 cups sugar
2 sticks (1 cup) butter
3 Tbsp water
1 Tbsp light corn syrup
1 tsp vanilla extract
2 cups (12 oz) semisweet chocolate chips
3/4 cup coarsely chopped peppermint candy canes

Preparation

1. Line a 13 x 9-in. baking pan with foil, letting foil extend about 2 in. above ends of pan. Lightly coat foil with nonstick spray.
2. In a heavy-bottom medium saucepan over medium heat, bring sugar, butter, water and corn syrup to a boil. Boil without stirring until a candy thermometer registers 300°F to 310°F. (Or drop a small amount into ice water. When mixture forms a brittle mass that snaps easily when pressed between fingers, it's ready.) Remove from heat and stir in vanilla (be careful, it splatters).
3. Pour into prepared pan. Wait 2 minutes, and sprinkle evenly with chocolate chips. When chips become shiny, about 2 minutes, spread over toffee. Sprinkle with chopped candy cane.

4. Refrigerate at least 2 hours until cold. Lift foil by ends onto a cutting board; break toffee in bite-size pieces.

Candy Cane Christmas Cookies

Ingredients:

1/2 cup granulated sugar
1/2 cup crushed peppermint candy canes or hard peppermint candies
1/2 cup (1 stick) salted butter or margarine, at room temperature
1/2 cup plain or butter-flavored shortening
1 cup confectioners- sugar
1 large egg
1 teaspoon vanilla extract
1/2 teaspoon peppermint extract
2 1/2 cups all-purpose flour
1/2 teaspoon liquid red food coloring

Preparation:

Adjust two racks to divide the oven into thirds. Preheat the oven to 375 degrees. Have ready two un-greased baking sheets. In a small bowl, mix the sugar with the crushed candy; set aside.

In a large bowl, with an electric mixer at medium-high speed, beat together the butter, shortening, confectioners-sugar, egg, vanilla, and peppermint extract until light and fluffy—2 or 3 minutes. With the mixer at medium-low speed, gradually add the flour, beating just until blended.

Remove half of the dough from the bowl and set aside on a sheet of waxed paper. To the dough remaining in the bowl, add the red food coloring and beat until evenly colored. (At this point each group of dough can be tightly wrapped separately in aluminum foil and refrigerated for up to a week or frozen for up to three months. If frozen, thaw in the refrigerator and bring to room temperature before proceeding.)

For each candy cane, scoop 1 teaspoonful of the plain dough and the same amount of pink dough. Roll each scoop between the palms of your hands to make a 4-inch rope. Twist the ropes together and shape into a candy cane. As they are made, arrange the canes on an un-greased baking sheet, spacing them about 1-inch apart.

Bake for about 9 minutes until firm to the touch and barely golden. Reverse the baking sheets on the racks and from front to back once during baking. The moment the cookies come from the oven, sprinkle each one with the sugar-and-peppermint mixture. With a wide turner, immediately transfer the cookies to wire racks to cool completely.

Store in a tightly covered container, separating the layers with sheets of waxed paper.

Christmas Candy Cane Fudge

Ingredients:

2/3 cup evaporated milk
1-2/3 cups granulated sugar
2 tbsp butter
1/2 tsp salt
2 cups miniature marshmallows
1.5 cups white chocolate chips
2 tsp mint extract
1/4 tsp red food coloring

Preparation:

1. Prepare an 8x8 pan by lining it with aluminum foil and spraying the foil with nonstick cooking spray.
2. In a medium saucepan over medium-high heat, combine the sugar, salt, evaporated milk, and butter and stir until the sugar melts.
3. Bring the mixture to a boil and boil, stirring constantly, for 5 minutes.
4. After 5 minutes, remove from the heat and stir in the marshmallows, white chocolate chips, and mint extract. Stir quickly and vigorously to incorporate all of the marshmallows and chocolate.
5. As soon as the candy is smooth, sprinkle drops of red food coloring over the top and stir once or twice, creating red swirls. Do not over-stir or the

candy will turn pink!
6. Immediately scrape the candy into the prepared pan. Allow to cool at room temperature or in the refrigerator until solid. To serve, cut into 1-inch squares.

The Legend of the
Candy Cane

In the Eighteenth Century somewhere in Europe any public display of Christianity was absolutely forbidden. No crosses or Bibles were allowed and the Christians were greatly oppressed. One old man, a candy maker by profession, was particularly distressed by this unfortunate situation. He loved the Lord with all of his heart and he was determined to share that love with the world. His heart especially went out to the children when Christmas drew near and no one was allowed to have a nativity scene on display in their homes.

One day in prayer he asked God to show him some way to make Christmas gifts for the children which would teach them the story of Christ.

The answer was the Candy Cane. The Candy Cane was in the shape of a shepherd's staff to show them that Jesus is our Shepherd and we are His flock. A sheep follows his own shepherd, knows his voice, trusts him and knows that he is totally safe with him. The sheep will follow no other shepherd but their own. This is how we are to be with Jesus if we truly follow Him (John 10:11; Psalm 23:1; Isaiah 40:11)

Upside down the Candy Cane was a "J", the first letter of Jesus' name. (Luke 1:31) It was made of hard candy to remind us that Christ is the rock of our salvation. The wide red stripes on the Candy Cane were to represent the blood He shed on the cross for each one of us so that we can have eternal life through Him. He redeemed us and cleansed us with His shed blood - the only thing that can wash away our sin. (Luke 22:20) .

The white stripes on a Candy Cane represented the virgin birth, sinless life and purity of our Lord. He is the only human being who ever lived on this earth who never committed a single sin. Even though He was tempted just as we are, He never sinned. (I Peter: 22)

The three narrow red stripes on the Candy Cane symbolized that by His stripes, or wounds, we are healed and they represent the Trinity - the Father, Son (Jesus) and Holy Spirit. Before the crucifixion Jesus was beaten; the crown of thorns was placed on His head; His back was raw from the whip. We are healed by those wounds. He bore our sorrows and by His stripes we are healed. (Isaiah 53:3)

The flavoring in the Candy Cane was peppermint, which is similar to hyssop. Hyssop is of the mint family and was used in Old Testament times for purification and sacrifice just as Jesus sacrificed His life for ours. (John 19:29; Psalm 51:7)

The old candy maker told the children that when we break our Candy Cane it reminds us that Jesus' body was broken for us. When we have communion it is a reminder of what He did for us. (I Cor: 11:24)

If we share our Candy Cane and give some to someone else in love it represents that same love of Jesus because He is to be shared with one another in love. (I John 4:7,8) God gave Himself to us when He sent Jesus. He loved us so much He wants us to spend eternal life with Him... which we can do if we accept Jesus in our hearts as Savior and Lord. (John 1:12; John 3:3,16)

Some people believe this story of the Candy Cane is just a legend. Others believe it really happened. We do not know for sure exactly how the Candy Cane was invented, but there is one thing for certain... it is an excellent symbol to remind us of Christ and His love for all of us.

Personal Cherished Christmas Memories, Traditions, Recipes, Notes & Keepsakes

The following pages are my personal Christmas gift to you! Settle comfortably into your favorite chair with a cup of *Christmas Tea* and record your wonderful memories, family traditions, cherished recipes passed down from favorite relatives, and stories that you remember from your *Christmas Past* so they will be forever immortalized in the pages of this book and lovingly preserved for all those dear ones down through the generations of family to come.

~Merry Christmas to All!~
xoxoxoxoxo

Sharyn McIntyre

Meet Me for Christmas Tea

Meet Me for Christmas Tea

Meet Me for Christmas Tea

Sharyn McIntyre

The Christmas Tea Series

"The Christmas Tea Series" is a series of Christmas stories all weaved with a familiar thread of holiday spirit...each one creating a different tapestry of inspiration focusing on life experiences through the eyes of characters in the midst of different stages of life and circumstances. There will be seven in all.

Traditional Christmas Tea is the story of an elderly lady who just celebrated her 90th birthday. She is forced to spend Christmas Eve all alone because of a powerful winter storm. Throughout the evening she reminisces about the days-gone-by, with cherished memories of special times spent with loved ones who are dear to her heart and memorable Christmas tea parties with her favorite Grandmother as she was growing up. As she falls asleep by the Christmas tree she is miraculously transported back to her Grandmother's kitchen of long ago, and to the most amazing *Christmas Tea Party* of her life.

In writing this story, it is my greatest desire to give hope to all those who are missing loved ones during the holiday season to reassure them that they will indeed see their precious loved ones once again some day.

Sharyn McIntyre

Christmas Tea with the Angels is centered on a sixteen year old girl who struggles with self-esteem issues and has given her personal power away to peer-pressure, social anxiety, and fear. As she falls asleep in her bed one night after a prayerful plea for help, she meets *THREE HEAV-ENLY HELPERS* who give her a whole new perspective on life, a heaping helping of courage, and a fresh new look at herself.

In writing this story, it is my deepest heart's desire to reach not only sixteen year old girls, but all girls and women of every age who have lost their sense of self-worth along the way somewhere, and to give them a brand new mirror in which to see the reflection of themselves as they really are.....Divinely created creatures perfectly designed with no mistakes in the process.....beautiful inside and out.

I sincerely hope that all those who find their way to **"The Christmas Tea Series"** will find great joy and inspiration from reading them.

Merry Christmas Eternal!

~Traditional Christmas Tea~
~Christmas Tea with the Angels~
~Meet Me for Christmas Tea~

Printed in the United States
135588LV00002B/14/P

9 781432 731595

2/05